ONE WILD NIGHT

[AN ENJOYING THE CHASE NOVELLA]

By Kirsty Moseley

Acknowledgements

Cover design by Mollie Wilson at M J Wilson Design. Mollie, thank you for making the stupid, vague and totally unhelpful idea I had look totally amazing!

Thank you to my amazing editors – Emily from Ruston Hutton, and Kristin at Hot Tree Editing.

Dedication

For no other reason other than she was beautiful, smart, strong, and loved the occasional F-bomb, I dedicate this one to my Auntie Pauline who sadly passed away this year.
Rest In Peace, Auntie, and know that you'll be missed and never forgotten. Xx

All proceeds and profits from the sale of this book or the ebook version will be donated to MacMillian Nurses for the wonderful work that they do. [Registered charity number: 261017]

Chapter One

I really couldn't procrastinate any longer. After taking one last look at my girl, I forced myself to walk out of the front door and down the stairs to the lobby. Tonight was my bachelor party, but I wasn't ready for it at all. If I was honest, all I really wanted to do tonight was lie on the sofa with my fiancée, Rosie, and watch TV, maybe catch a little early night so I could ravage her body. However, my best friend, Ashton Taylor, had decided I needed to go out and celebrate my last night of freedom.

As I stood in the lobby waiting for him to arrive, a bad feeling settled in the pit of my stomach. I had no idea where we were going or what we were going to be doing tonight – all I knew was that when Ashton had gotten married a few years back, I had taken my best man duties seriously, and of course had teased the shit out of him all night long. Tonight was probably going to be payback.

As the front door swung open and Ashton strutted in with a shit-eating grin on his face, I groaned loudly. He was wearing a black T-shirt that read: 'Best man of the pussy-whipped party' on the front.

"You ready for this, Nate?" he asked.

"Seriously? You're wearing that?" I asked, pointing down at his chest.

He laughed and nodded, throwing his arm around my shoulder. "This is going to be one wild night, but don't worry; I'll get you so drunk you won't even remember it in the morning," he assured me, leading me out of the building

I sighed deeply. I had a feeling I was going to live to regret ever meeting him by the time morning came. This was probably going to be the most painfully embarrassing night of my twenty-five years of life.

When I stepped out of the door, I already wanted to cry. They were all standing there, all of my friends, waiting for me in front of the minibus we were obviously using tonight. They cheered and chinked beer bottles, grinning like morons even though it was barely past lunchtime. All of my friends were decked out in T-shirts like Ashton's, but instead, theirs read: 'Team member of the pussy-whipped party' on it. My dad, Evan, was there, too; his said 'I'm the daddy'. Even George, my soon-to-be father-in-law, wore one that said 'Father of the bride' on the front.

Something flew towards my face, so I caught it quickly, looking down at my own T-shirt. 'Groom' had been printed on the front, but they'd crossed it out and written 'Bride's Bitch' there instead. I flipped it over and looked at the back. 'It's my last night being single, please spank me'.

I closed my eyes and shook my head. "I hate you guys," I grumbled, but my meagre protests just made them cheer and chink their bottles again.

"Let the bacheloring begin!" Ashton enthused, grinning.

I sighed and decided just to go with it. I knew I was in for strippers, drinking, probably some embarrassing display of being tied up naked somewhere, and whatever else could come out of Ashton Taylor's warped little mind.

My friends all started piling on the minibus, and my gaze settled on the large sign that had been hand-painted onto an old bed sheet and stuck to the side of the bus. "Son of a bitch," I grumbled under my breath, following reluctantly behind them all and climbing on the bus. As I stripped out of my nice shirt I'd chosen for tonight and pulled on the party shirt instead, I smiled apologetically at the driver who had obviously been paid to ferry us around all night long. No doubt, he would see some embarrassing antics tonight before he dropped us all home.

I glanced down the bus, seeing everyone properly for the first time. On top of there being my best friend, dad and soon to be father-in-law, there was also eight other guys. All of whom I was close friends with; one of them I knew from work.

My eyes settled on Seth; he was grinning like an idiot. "I'm guessing you were the one who made the huge 'pussy mobile' sign on the side of the van?" I asked, raising one eyebrow at him. Out of all of my friends, he was the one who was most similar to what I used to be before I met Rosie and settled down. He was a player. He was the only one who didn't understand my desire to marry the girl of my dreams. To Seth, getting married was like the death penalty.

He grinned and raised his beer bottle to me in toast. "You guessed right."

Nodding, I looked around and immediately spotted a case full of beer on the front seats, along with various other bottles of alcohol and a couple of duffle bags. My curiosity spiked immediately. Part of me wanted to know what was in the bags; the other part, the more rational part, told me I needed to be drunk before I found out.

I plucked out a beer and popped the cap, raising it in cheers to the group who were watching me excitedly. "To getting married," I toasted.

"To the last fling before the ring," Seth countered, raising his bottle, too.

I rolled my eyes and George, Rosie's dad, cleared his throat, raising a warning eyebrow.

I smiled back reassuringly. "Don't worry, George, the only sex I'm having tonight will be some phone sex with your daughter later," I joked, winking at him, which just made him groan and shake his head in disapproval.

I plopped down in the seat next to Ashton. He grinned and tapped his bottle against mine. "To getting so hammered that we have no recollection of this in the morning," he said, grinning wickedly and sipping his beer.

I closed my eyes and tried not to think about what I had let myself in for with these guys. Was getting married really worth this afternoon and night of torture? Rosie's face popped into my head, and the face of her little four-year-old son, DJ. They sure as hell were worth all this torture, worth a lot more, too. I'd literally already walked through fire for them, so this little night out would seem like a walk in the park compared to that. I laughed despite myself when everyone in the minibus – including the driver – started to sing, 'I'm getting married in the morning'.

By the time we pulled up at our desired destination, I was already onto my second beer and my nerves were starting to dissipate. I'd decided to roll with it; they could do their worst to me, so long as I made it to the church for 1 p.m. the following day. I was only planning to go through this whole wedding thing once anyway, so at least this night of celebrating would be a one-off.

As we pulled into the parking lot, George stood up and gasped. "I thought this was a joke! I thought when you suggested this, you were just fooling around!" he practically shouted as the colour drained from his face.

Confused, I turned to look at where we were. An airfield. Panic made me jerk in my seat. "Please tell me we're staying in this country. If I'm late tomorrow, then Rosie's gonna have my balls! Well, actually, she *wouldn't* have my balls, and that would be worse," I joked, looking at Ashton pleadingly.

He grinned and patted my knee. "We're staying in this country, just maybe a little higher than usual," he confirmed, waggling his eyebrows at me and pointing out of the window.

Looking in the direction he was pointing, a smile crept onto my face. I loved anything sporty or dangerous. I turned back to George and gave him a wicked grin. "What's up, York, you scared of a little parachute jump?" I teased, laughing as he flipped me the finger.

"Shut up, Nate," he answered, flopping back into his chair with his eyes closed. My dad slung an arm around his shoulder, talking to him reassuringly.

I laughed and turned back to Ashton, my partner in crime, the guy who was usually at my side when crazy stuff started happening. "This is gonna be awesome!"

It took a long time for them to run through the training stuff, how to land and what to do. Luckily, it was a tandem jump, so the guy strapped to our backs would be doing all of the work. All we had to remember was to keep our hands out of the way, enjoy falling 12,000 feet from an aeroplane, and pray the parachute would open.

Once the initial training was done, we met the people who would be jumping with us. I shook the hand of my guy – a huge guy called Blane. I looked over to Seth to see him frowning at my dad. When my eyes went that way, I spotted why he was frowning. My dad's instructor was a woman, a pretty one, too.

"No offence, Blane, but how come I get you strapped to my ass instead of her?" I asked, nudging him with my elbow.

He laughed and rolled his eyes. "You'd be surprised how many times a day I get asked that. Anyway, tell your friend not to bother, she doesn't bat for his team," he replied, nodding at Seth who was now trying his luck, complimenting her on her red jumpsuit and asking her if she came here often.

I grinned and slapped Seth on the back of his head, making him shoot me a dirty look. "You lucked out, buddy. You got the wrong body parts for that one."

His frown deepened. "Dammit, really? That sucks," he grumbled.

"Life isn't always fair," I answered. I flicked my eyes over to George, who was sitting on the bench, his head in his hands. "All right, George? You don't have to do this, you know," I said, sitting next to him and patting his back. As father-in-laws went, I got a good one; he was an incredibly nice guy.

He took a deep breath and looked at me with watery eyes. "I don't want to look like a punk in front of your friends. They'll be teasing me about it all through the wedding," he whined.

I smiled. "Just come in the plane with us. If you don't want to jump, then don't," I suggested. He nodded, closing his eyes and moving his lips as if he was saying a silent prayer.

When we were all set, we boarded the aeroplane. It took a while for us to reach the right height, but when we did, the instructors came over and started strapping everyone to their fronts. George looked like he was going into a state of panic.

Rick, one of my friends, was bending right forward, theatrically sticking his head between his legs. "Rick, what you up to, dude?" I asked, laughing to myself. That looked like a weird position to be in.

He raised his head and looked at me. "Kissing my ass goodbye," he answered, laughing. We all burst out laughing; even George had a couple of chuckles – until the door of the plane opened and suddenly the laughter died down.

I watched as we lined up into the order that we'd drawn straws for back on the ground. I was fourth, after George. He was mumbling something as he sat in front of me. I squeezed his shoulder, trying to reassure him as we watched Adam and then Wayne throw themselves out of the plane, laughing as they did it. All of my friends were thrill-seekers, just like I was. Bungee jumping, rock-climbing, car racing, we did it all.

Needing to mark the moment, I pulled out my cell phone and recorded a video of George as he waited to go. He was shaking his head, saying he didn't want to go, clinging to the side of the door as his instructor scooted him forward so his legs were dangling off the edge. He was literally screaming like a teenage girl at a Justin Bieber concert. The instructor looked back at me to see if he should go or not. I grinned and nodded, pushing him forward at the same time as he scooted forward and threw himself and my soon-to-be father-in-law out of the plane. I heard him screaming, and screaming and screaming. Even over the roar of the plane engines, I could hear it, and I just couldn't stop laughing.

I looked back as Ashton as I shoved the cell phone back into my pocket. "That one's going on Facebook when we get home," I confirmed, slapping him a high-five.

Then it was my turn. This was a first for me. I'd never actually jumped out of a plane before. I started to get nervous. I tried not to think about my chute not opening and us plummeting to the ground. I tried not to imagine the feeling of knowing you were going to die and being powerless to stop it. I tried, but it just kept flooding my brain.

Blane tapped my shoulder. "You ready?" he shouted over the gusts of wind that were whipping around my ears. I nodded, knowing if I spoke, I would sound somewhat like George did a minute earlier. I knew Ashton would be recording me, waiting for me to scream like a pansy, too. There was no way I was giving him the satisfaction of that.

I gulped as he scooted us forward, my legs dangling out of the plane; the wind was whipping about my face making it a little hard to breathe. A quick glance over my shoulder at Ashton confirmed what I'd suspected – he was recording me on his cell phone, too.

I gulped and forced a smile, whilst silently repeating the word 'fuck' over and over in my head. I gave him the thumbs up and then Blane shifted us again. Then I was falling, free-falling from 12,000 feet.

The free-fall lasted for less than a minute, and the whole time I could feel the adrenalin rushing through my system. My heart crashed in my chest, but I actually loved it. Suddenly, the chute opened and the straps tightened around my body as we jerked upwards. I laughed and held onto my straps as I looked around. From up here you could see everything, the fields below, the blue sky. It was majestic.

Below us, the other guys were all coasting on their parachutes, too. George was grinning now. He was pointing out things to his partner, smiling broadly. I turned my head back and could see other chutes, too, belonging to the people behind me. I sighed happily. Maybe my bachelor party was going to be fun after all; it was definitely off to a good start.

When we hit the ground about five minutes later, I grinned and let Blane unbuckle me before I stood up and looked around. They were gathering off to one side, so we moved out of the way and watched the others land, too. George was literally raving about it, hopping from one foot to the other, suggesting we go again.

As soon as Seth hit the ground and was unbuckled, he was searching the floor, kicking his feet, looking for something, frowning. "What you lost, Seth? Your balls?" I called, laughing as George slapped my back in congratulations. Seth looked up at me, his face pure horror and I immediately tensed up, thinking something bad had happened. I ran to his side, kicking at the ground, too, looking for whatever he'd lost. "What is it?" I asked, watching as he bent to pick up a rock before tossing back down again.

"Dude, I dropped my fucking phone!" he whined, shaking his head dramatically. "Do you have any idea how many girls' numbers I had stored in there? Damn it, I had this hot little chick in there who I met last night, I was supposed to call her and arrange to take her out. Christ, she was a freaking gymnast, too!" he moaned, kicking at the ground again.

I burst out laughing. "A phone, really?" I rolled my eyes. "Why didn't you put it in your jeans pocket?" I asked.

He closed his eyes and frowned. "I was taking a video of George screaming," he explained, shaking his head. "It's gone now though. I was gonna YouTube that sucker!"

I laughed and patted my pocket. "I got one, don't worry. We'll stich him up real good," I assured him, winking conspiratorially. "Can't do much about the gymnast though, I'm afraid," I added, smirking at him as he groaned again. I looped my arm around his neck, getting him in a headlock and dragging him off to the side with everyone else. "Time for drinking now, or are we doing something else?" I asked. Ashton just smiled at me wickedly.

I stood at the mirror and winced. I looked like a dick, a complete and utter dick. "Seriously, what are we, three?" I called over the top of the dressing room curtain.

"Three-and-a-half," Ashton called back, laughing.

I groaned and raked my eyes down myself in the full-length mirror. Black pants, black shirt with gold stitching on it, black cummerbund. I looked like a serious prick. I pulled on the mask that covered my eyes then plopped on my black hat and sheathed my sword. Zorro. I was going out tonight dressed as fucking Zorro.

I whipped back the curtain and walked into the middle of the room, looking around the fancy-dress shop that we were all situated in. Some of my friends whooped and whistled as a joke, so I did a little twirl, flicking out my cape, laughing at how stupid I felt. *I seriously better not remember this in the morning!*

We were mostly all dressed as superheroes tonight. This was apparently my dad's idea, and he'd called ahead reserving all of the outfits for tonight. My dad was dressed as Iron Man. Wayne was Spiderman. Russell, my forty-five-year-old teammate, was dressed as Luke Skywalker. I burst out laughing as I saw my father-in-law. He'd apparently not wanted to go for a superhero tonight; instead, he opted to go as a 60s pimp. He was decked out in a purple velvet suit, fake gold jewellery and a wide-brimmed, purple velvet hat with leopard print trim on everything. He grinned at me and pulled on the collar of his suit jacket, pouting, trying to look like a pimp – but not pulling it off in the slightest.

"George, you are way too funny. This is where Rosie gets her craziness from!" I chuckled, shaking my head as I snapped a couple of photos of him while he posed with my dad.

Someone slapped my shoulder so I looked around to see Ashton had come out of his changing cubicle. He was Batman. I laughed and elbowed him in the fake rubber abs and shook my head. "Very sexy," I commented, rolling my eyes at him.

"Later we'll see who would win if Batman were to fight Zorro like you always wondered," he suggested, grinning wickedly. "I've hired a wrestling ring and we're gonna see which superhero, or pimp daddy, would come out on top of a superhero battle." He rubbed his hands together excitedly. This was something we'd discussed a lot whilst drunk over the years – which superhero was the best. For me, Zorro kicked ass every time.

I laughed and looked back at George, who was busy strutting in his suit and three-inch platforms. "Just don't hurt my father-in-law. Rosie would bitch me out big time if he couldn't walk her down the aisle tomorrow." I laughed at George and shook my head. "You look *way* too comfortable in that outfit, George."

He grinned and nodded. "I used to wear this kind of thing all the time when I was a kid."

I frowned. "Just how old are you exactly?" I asked, laughing.

"Still young enough to kick your ass," he said, shrugging and smirking at me.

"Leave that fighting talk for later," I suggested, grinning.

Ashton looked around everyone. "Are we all ready?"

I shrugged, looking for anyone that was missing. There were only eleven of us here. "Where's Rick?" I asked, frowning. We all turned back towards the changing rooms; there was one curtain still shut. "Rick, you ready, bud?"

A loud groan came from behind the curtain. "I'm not going," he replied, his voice muffled.

Ashton and I both exchanged a quizzical glance before heading over to the offending curtain that was shielding the last member of my 'pussy-whipped party'. Ashton pulled it back quickly and there stood Rick, dressed in a full, skintight Superman outfit.

His eyes widened, as he looked over first me, and then Ashton. Suddenly, his brow furrowed and he shook his head as his hand shot to his crotch which was pretty much exposed in his tight and revealing outfit. He looked around the group

15

standing behind me, consisting of The Green Lantern, Captain America, Optimus Prime and a couple more.

"Oh, man, this blows! Why do I have to be the only one in actual spandex? You guys get muscle suits, and I get spandex? Someone up there hates me. And, to top it all off, it's freaking cold outside!" he whined, shaking his head fiercely. "I'm not going out in this. There must be something else," he stated, looking around quickly.

Ashton grinned and rolled his eyes. "You're going as Superman! There wouldn't be much of a battle if Superman wasn't there, now, would there?" he teased, slinging his arm around Rick's shoulder and guiding him out of the changing room. Ashton looked down at his watch. "Now it's time for the pièce de résistance! It took me forever to arrange this, so you'd better appreciate it!" he said, grinning at me excitedly.

I frowned at him quizzically. "What are we doing?"

"You'll see," he replied, as the other boys whooped and hollered excitedly.

Tears of joy stung my eyes. This was easily one of the best things that had ever happened to me. I was snapping photos like a madman as *the* Jimmy Meddler walked down the carpeted aisle towards the wrestling ring where we were all standing. I couldn't breathe properly, and I was seriously making myself look like a punk. Luckily for me, everyone had the same awed expressions as I did; my dad was actually covering his mouth and jumping up and down.

We were in the famous recording studios where my childhood heroes smacked the shit out of each other for our entertainment. I was literally standing in the ring where my heroes had stood, watching as the most incredible wrestler in the world walked towards me. His jet-black hair was covered by a red bandana the same as usual, and a black vest with 'The Meddler' was covering his muscled chest. My mouth dropped open in awe as he climbed into the ring, standing there at a mammoth six-feet-eight. At age fifty-nine, he still took my breath away.

When he made a growling sound and tore his shirt in half, throwing it at my feet, I just about lost it. Now it was my turn to scream like a pre-pubescent girl who had just been hugged by Harry Styles. Ashton clapped me on the back, grinning like an idiot. We'd spent many an hour when we were young and stupid trying to re-enact some of this guy's moves. He probably loved him just as much as I did.

"This is a wedding gift, from me to you," he stated, snapping photos of Jimmy Meddler on his cell phone.

I stepped forward and prayed my voice would work when I spoke to the man I always wanted to grow up as when I was a kid. "Oh, man, I'm your biggest fan! I was a total Meddlermaniac when I was younger; I still am. I've watched all your movies at least a hundred times. I had them all on video back before DVDs were even invented. You. Are. Awesome," I gushed, raking my eyes over him, shaking my head in bewilderment.

He grinned and held out his hand to me. "You must be Nate Peters. It's nice to meet you. I always wanted to meet my biggest fan," he joked, laughing his booming laugh that just made my eyes widen as I tried not to squeal and throw myself at him for a hug.

I giggled. Actually giggled like a little girl. I knew I needed to grow a pair, but I just couldn't. Jimmy Meddler was standing in front of me; this was a dream come true. *Christ, I love my best friend!*

"Can I get a photo with you? My fiancée has a little thing for you, too. Right, George?" I said, turning to look at my soon-to-be father-in-law.

He nodded in confirmation. "Oh, yeah, she used to have posters of you and everything."

Jimmy grinned and wrapped his arm around me, pulling me to his side. I laughed and tilted my head back to look at him. *Jeez, he's tall!* I was six-foot, but he even made me feel small.

"So, is your girl hot? Maybe I should meet her," Jimmy teased as we posed for photos.

I laughed. "I really need to kick your ass if you're thinking about making a move on my girl.

She'll love me even more when I tell her I gave The Meddler the smackdown," I replied, laughing.

He raised one eyebrow and pulled back looking at me challengingly. "In your dreams, Zorro. You're not big enough to smackdown Jimmy Meddler."

"Meaning no disrespect to you here, Mr Meddler, but when I tell my girl about this tomorrow, you're having your ass handed to you regardless of the outcome of tonight," I joked, winking at him.

He burst out laughing and slung his arm around my shoulder, almost making my knees buckle under the sheer weight of it. "You're all right, Zorro. You're all right," he replied, nodding.

"The Meddler has agreed to teach us some moves and ref the superhero battle," Ashton said, grinning excitedly.

I groaned as I lay on my back, gasping for breath for probably the eighth time in three minutes. We'd been play-fighting it out for ages. Jimmy Meddler was showing us his moves; how to fall without getting hurt, and showing us the tricks to being a professional wrestler. I was having the time of my life. The only thing that would make this better was if Rosie and DJ were here, too. We'd had the superhero battle already, but none of us were taking it seriously because we were all too eager to get in the ring with The Meddler. Ashton and I had got to the end, beating everyone to prove that Zorro and Batman were the biggest badasses of all heroes, but we both quit before seeing who would win. Apparently, we were short on time because they wanted the ring cleared because there was an actual show being filmed in an hour.

The Meddler grinned and pushed himself off me, holding down a hand to help me to my feet. I rubbed at my back, groaning as I looked at him in awe. I looked back to Ashton. "Please tell me you recorded that! Jimmy fucking Meddler just did a powerslam on me!" I cried excitedly.

He nodded quickly. "I got it. Do a suplex now!" he said eagerly.

Jimmy laughed and shook his head. "That's enough for today. The poor guy is getting married tomorrow, that's enough punishment for one lifetime," he protested, grinning at me.

I held my hand out and slapped him a high-five. My whole body hurt, but that was so totally worth it. "You have just made my bachelor party. This was freaking awesome! Thanks so much for doing this," I gushed.

He laughed and strutted over to his bag he'd dumped in the corner. When he turned back to me, he held out his ripped T-shirt and a signed photo of himself. I gasped and practically snatched it out of his hands.

"Here, I got you this, too," he said, turning and taking something off Ashton. I held out my hand for whatever it was. This was just too much. Meeting Jimmy Meddler, getting his ripped shirt. This night was incredible!

Something wet and hard dropped into my hand. I tore my eyes away from his autograph long enough to look what it was. I frowned when I saw a bright pink dildo in the palm of my hand.

What the hell?

"Er, thanks. Umm… what's that for?" I asked, shaking my head and laughing at the randomness of it.

All the boys were laughing, laughing so hard they were clutching their sides. Ashton was bent in half, his hands on his knees as he gasped for breath. Even Jimmy was laughing his big booming laugh.

I frowned, getting even more confused. "I don't think my girl needs one of these. I can take care of that," I stated, still trying to work out what they were all in hysterics for.

That was when I saw what Ashton was holding. Realisation suddenly washed over me as I tried to open my hand to drop the offending object. I turned my hand over, but it was already welded to my palm.

My asshole friends had just superglued a bright pink dildo to the palm of my hand, and Jimmy Meddler, my childhood hero, was the one who actually passed it to me.

"You bitches suck," I groaned, closing my eyes and imagining walking into the ER asking for them to remove this.

Ashton reached out and grabbed my wrist, flipping my hand over and poking at the bottom of it carefully. That was the moment I really started to hate my friends.

Apparently, it was a *flashing*, bright pink dildo. Just pure awesomeness.

Chapter Two

The assholes insisted we were to stop at every bar and do a shot; then, when we got to the minibus that was at the end of the road, we would apparently go to the hospital to get the dildo removed. By the time we made it past five bars, I was actually growing accustomed to having it stuck to my hand. It was like a glow stick, and I was moronically waving it over my head to the beat of the music as we laughed and waited for our drinks.

It was only about eight in the evening, and I was already wasted. When I flicked my eyes around, my vision seemed to take a second or two to catch up with the movement. It was a little disorientating, but considering I had been drunk thousands of times since I was legal to drink – and even before I was legal, too – I could cope with it. However, I could just as easily stop drinking and go home to bed. I could do what I told George I was going to do earlier and call his daughter up for some nasty phone time. She went crazy for that kind of thing. That was definitely being added to my plan at some point in the night.

Ashton grinned and pulled a cell phone out of his pocket. "Time for some calls," he chirped. I laughed. This was something we hadn't done in a while. Prank calls. He held the phone out, grinning. It wasn't his phone, we had bought a cheap one specifically for this purpose; the number had been blocked and didn't receive incoming calls. It was only ever used for our entertainment purposes. "Who wants to go first?" he asked, flicking his eyes around the group.

Seth took the phone out of his hand, laughing. "Me!" He dialled in a number; I knew it would be one of his family. That was our thing: we each had to call a member of our family and prank them for at least one minute. It could either be one phone call, or a combination of several calls, as long as they lasted over a minute and were all to the same person. If they guessed it was us, then you lost and had to down a shot from the 'fish bowl'. The fish bowl was disgusting. We literally bought one of every drink and mixed them all together in a huge glass bowl or jug. I winced when I saw Ashton was currently pouring a glass of JD and

Coke, and followed it with a Malibu and pineapple juice, then a whiskey chaser or two and some other coloured shots, which made the whole thing turn a blue-green colour. I prayed I didn't get caught out because that drink was going to taste vile.

My dad and George had obviously never heard of this game before. My dad shot me an accusing look. "This is why I get dodgy calls every couple of weeks?" he asked. "That one from the Thai laundry factory that told me if I didn't come and collect my clothes, they were going to take me to court and charge me rent for storing them for so long? That was you?"

I burst out laughing. That call had been awesome. I'd managed to keep him on the line for a good five minutes while he explained he'd never even heard of 'I bang anything laundry services'. I'd had him on speaker while he shouted the fake name out, telling me to take him to court, that his son was a cop and that he didn't even care.

Ashton slapped me a high-five, laughing his ass off. "That was the best call ever. Nate still has the record for that one," he said, nodding at me proudly.

Seth waved his hand to get our attention and held one finger to his lips, signalling for us to be quiet. I grinned and chewed on my lip, trying not to laugh too loud and ruin it for him. "Hello, am I talking to a Mrs Monterary?" he asked. I shook my head; he was pranking his mother. "Mrs Monterary, this is Special Agent Pratt. I'm calling to inform you about a pending lawsuit against you for copyright infringement. We have traced over 20GB of illegal downloading from your IP address. As you are most probably aware, it is a crime to download pirated movies, music and literature. A process server from my department will be at your house within the next twenty-four hours to impound your computer and any other devices which are found to contain illegally downloaded material," he said, holding up his hand for one of those fist punches.

My dad leant over to me. "This is a lot funnier when you're on the other side of it," he whispered, laughing as he watched Seth, who was currently arguing with his mom about how they can't be wrong because his department never made mistakes.

After less than a minute, he groaned and looked defeated. "Damn it! How did you know it was me?" he whined, closing his eyes as Ashton poured out a shot glass full to the brim with the toxic-looking drink. "Yeah, yeah. I'll see you Sunday for dinner, okay? Yeah, love you, too, Mom," he replied, snapping the phone shut and sliding it across the bar to me. He sighed and took the glass, taking a couple of deep breaths before chugging it down, gagging a couple of times as he did it.

I picked up the phone and dialled in Toni's number; she was Rosie's sister, and I'd never pranked her before, so I had a pretty good chance of pulling this off.

When Toni answered, I grinned and launched into my prepared spiel. "Hi there, this is Wayne Kerr from Radio Heat. In thirty seconds, you're going to be live on the radio because your ex-partner, David, has answered three questions correctly and is currently in the running to win a luxury vacation to Barbados. When we get back on the air, I'm going to ask you three general knowledge questions. If you get them correct, then both of you will win the vacation. Oh, and please don't use offensive language. We will be live on the radio to over twelve million people," I lied.

I heard her gasp and mumble something off the line. "Oh, my God, seriously?" she cried.

"If you could just hold the line for thirty seconds," I added before putting my hand over the mouthpiece and laughing as she started rambling about how she didn't want to go on the radio. She kept asking how I had got her number, had David given it to me, why had he chosen her to answer questions with him. I didn't respond to any of it, just looked at my watch, waiting for my minute to be up, smirking at Ashton confidently.

Suddenly, I heard a familiar voice. "Nate Peters, you had better not be pranking my little sister," Rosie said down the line.

I laughed. *Aww, screw it.* "Hey, Stripes. How did you know it was me?" I asked, rolling my eyes.

"Wayne Kerr, sounds like wanker. I knew it had to be you as soon as she said who was calling," she responded, laughing.

I grinned sheepishly. That was another rule; we always had to throw in something obvious to give them a clue. Seth had used Special Agent Pratt; I thought my selection was a pretty good name to use – obviously not. "Damn, you got me. Thanks for that, now I have to drink something that's gonna make me sick in the morning," I replied, wincing as Ashton poured me a drink.

"Go play your boy games and leave us alone. We're having a long conversation about you and you're interrupting," she teased. Rosie had her girls over with her tonight, including both of our moms, our sisters, and Ashton's wife, Anna.

"I hope it's all good stuff," I responded.

She laughed. "Not really. You're not exactly a good boy, are you, Officer Peters?" she flirted.

I groaned when she called me that. She knew just how to get me excited. I blew out a big breath and shook my head; I really had met my match with Rosie. "Right, whatever. Try not to miss me too much tonight," I stated, wishing I was back there with her so I could see the smile I knew she'd be sporting. "See you tomorrow."

"Yep. G'night. Have fun," she replied before cutting me off, obviously wanting to get back to her girlie gossiping and drinking.

Ashton squeezed my shoulder. "Did you forget Toni was with Rosie tonight?" he asked, rolling his eyes. I nodded in response. If I had remembered that, I definitely wouldn't have called her; Rosie sussed me too easily. "That was a good one, though; I bet that would have worked if she wasn't there."

I nodded in agreement. She definitely had no clue it was me. Damn my fiancée for knowing me too well! I gripped the glass in my only free hand and mentally counted to three, trying to psych myself up to drinking it. On three, I swallowed the contents as quickly as I could. I heaved as it slid down my throat, putting my other hand up to cover my mouth, but then heaving again when the dildo poked me up the nose.

"My turn!" Ashton chirped. He took the phone and grinned. "I'm calling my father-in-law," he announced, tapping in the number.

There were collective gasps from the group. Ashton's father-in-law was the President of the United States. Not really someone you should be prank calling, but then again, he adored Ashton so if he found him out then he would probably laugh it off anyway. I had no idea how he was going to get hold of him at this time of night, but then again he probably had a private number for him.

"Good evening, sir," Ashton sang in an extremely camp voice. "I'm calling in response to your email we received today. Sorry to call you so late in the day but I really needed to clarify a couple of details with you. Your request was very specific, and it's going to take me a good few hours to arrange what you wanted."

I looked at him curiously, wondering what on earth he was up to.

"Well, I got your number from the email you sent us, sir. This is the user LadiesLoveOral?" Ashton continued, not giving him a chance to reply. "Well, like I was saying, we received your email about the male escort you wanted. You say you want a blond man of Chinese origin, between the ages of eighteen and twenty-five. Well I can certainly arrange that for you, but the one blue eye and one brown thing really has us stumped. Would you be disappointed with the escort wearing coloured contacts? You can get some very real-looking ones nowadays."

I was in hysterics just imagining President Spencer listening to this. Ashton was probably going to get in some deep shit for this.

"What do you mean I have the wrong number? This was the number provided on the email. Sir? Hello, are you there?" Ashton said. He pulled the phone away from his ear and laughed. "He hung up on me. How long do I have left?"

"About twenty seconds," Seth announced, laughing and looking at his watch.

Ashton dialled again, putting the phone to his ear. "I'm so sorry, sir. The cleaners are in the building, and I think one of them must have knocked out the power cord with the vacuum," he said. I could see he was struggling to stop himself from laughing as he listened to the response. I would imagine President Spencer couldn't exactly just tell a stranger down the line who he was; after all, he didn't want a guy who ran an escort company to have his private phone number.

"Hmm, well, that *is* strange. I have your number here clear as day. Your order for the escort was requested to attend a high-class function with you next Thursday. Are you sure maybe someone there didn't request him? Maybe your wife or girlfriend was using your email and credit card? Our fee of $2,000 has already been paid in full so maybe she was ordering our services on your behalf?" Ashton suggested. He choked on his laughter as he shook his head. "No, sir. I'm not suggesting your wife has a fetish for Chinese men."

Seth tapped his watch, signalling his time was up, and Ashton pumped the air in celebration.

"Oh, my goodness. I've misdialled! That should be a four, not a one. Oh, dear, I have fat fingers. I'm sorry to bother you, have a pleasant evening." He disconnected the call and did a little victory dance on the spot.

"Oh, that was freaking awesome!" I chirped, shaking my head in awe. The only thing that would have made it better was seeing the President's face when he was on the call.

Ashton did a little bow before holding the phone out to my dad. "Evan, up for a little prank?"

My dad nodded and took the phone, seeming ridiculously eager. I watched the keypad as he dialled; it looked like my Aunt Lucy's number. He was laughing already. There was no way he was going to pull this off; he had no poker face at all. "Pizza Italiano, may I taker your order?" he asked in a heavy Italian accent, closing his eyes and trying not to laugh down the phone. "I'm sorry, ma'am, but you just call me. Can I taker your order?" he asked, adding in wrong words for emphasis. "I not call you. I just pick up the phone and you were there. Did you want I make you a pizza or not?"

I shook my head. This one was an old one, but a good one; he would never make it last a minute though; this was a rookie mistake.

She hung up on him, so he dialled her again. "Pizza Italiano, can I taker your order?" he repeated when she answered the phone. "It's you again? Look, I have very busy restaurant. I can't be dealing with time-wasters. Did you want to place order for pizza or not?" he snapped, grinning like an idiot. Aunt Lucy was a little fiery at times, I would imagine she was letting rip on the phone because he was covering the mouth piece, laughing.

She obviously hung up on him after her rant, so he dialled her again. "Pizza Italiano." He gasped dramatically. "Look, I don't know who you are, but if this is some kind of joke, then it's not funny. I have a business to run, so if you keep calling and wasting my time then I'm going to contact the police!" His Italian accent slipped so he sounded just like himself. He immediately slapped his forehead and groaned. "Yeah, sorry, Lucy. I know, I know, I should be leading by example and whatnot. Hey, don't blame me, I'm not the reason he turned out the way he did!" he protested, punching me on the arm. "Yeah, I'll tell him. See you tomorrow at the wedding," he added. He turned to me and rolled his eyes. "She got me. Pass me the drink," he groaned.

I patted his shoulder and smiled sympathetically. "Don't take it to heart, old man. I called her last week when I went out with Ashton," I said, chuckling darkly.

He groaned and downed the glass of the vile green drink before visibly shuddering. He wiped his mouth on the back of his hand and looked at his empty glass. "Actually, it's not that bad. I might make your mother one of those one day. She likes cocktails. They make her a little dirty," he stated, nodding appreciatively and winking at Seth, who held up his hand for a high-five while both Ashton and I just looked at him in disgust.

After everyone had a turn with a call, the fish bowl was empty, so we made our way to another bar that was next door. The end was in sight now; I could see the minibus, it was at the end of the road waiting for us. I had probably three more bars and then I could get the god-awful pink sex toy removed from my hand at the ER. Maybe then, people would stop staring at me like some sort of pervert gone wild.

Everyone at the ER was very amused with my situation. Nurses and doctors filed into my room one after the other, claiming they were just picking up something, like a chart or a spare bandage or something. In reality, news had probably travelled quickly about the prick dressed as Zorro who had accidentally super-glued a flashing pink vibrator to his hand.

One nurse, a grey-haired, stern-faced looking woman, actually clicked her tongue at me and muttered something that sounded very much like, "disgraceful and you should be ashamed of yourself," as she left the room.

I was in there for probably less than twenty minutes; of course, we were bumped to the front of the line when people saw I was with Ashton, a guy famous in his own right for being part of 'Annaton', celebrity couple, and the President's son-in-law. For the speedy visit, I was very grateful.

I wasn't as grateful, however, for the fact that my friends wouldn't let the doctor remove it without me posing for a photo with him. Apparently, it was for blackmailing situations in the future. Seth actually told me that if I didn't let him bang my little sister, he would print up posters of it and deliver them to my boys I worked with. To be honest, though, it was an empty threat considering that Russell, aka the Luke Skywalker impersonator tonight, was out with us and had already snapped his own photo, which I was sure, would be passed around at work anyway. I was fully expecting to get back from my honeymoon to find mugs, posters, plates and whatever else he could get printed up with my face and a pink ladies toy displayed on it.

Finally, we were done, so we went to get on with the binge-drinking tour. All of us were singing as we walked down the street. George was whining that he wanted to dance and wanted to hit a club already, but everyone else protested it was too early for that. Instead, we headed into a sports bar that was not too far away from the hospital.

As we walked, I flicked my eyes around and frowned. It was Friday night, it should have been busy; instead, I only saw the barman and two other people in there. They were standing up at the bar talking. If it wasn't for them, then I would have thought the place was closed for business. It was a crappy place, dirty, old and dark. I wasn't actually too surprised people chose to spend their money elsewhere.

The boys all headed in ahead of us. Ashton and I were bringing up the rear, laughing at some joke I'd just told him about a unicorn and an angel that got trapped in an elevator. Suddenly, fingers bit into my arm making me wince despite the alcohol that I had sloshing through my system.

"We need to leave!" Ashton hissed in my ear.

Leave? What on earth for? We've only just walked through the door! I turned back to look at him; his eyes were wide and his jaw tight. He was looking off to my right, his fingers still digging into my forearm. "Dude, what's up with you?" I asked, flicking my eyes in the direction he was looking. Immediately, I spotted what was wrong with him. There was a tall brunette girl standing over at the bar, laughing with her friend. I recognised her immediately. It was the girl from Long Beach – the one who we had our doubts of sexuality over and vowed never to talk about. Ashton's little brush with the other side when we were eighteen and drunk. I burst out laughing, and his grip tightened on me.

"We need to leave, right now!" he growled, shaking his head and forcibly trying to drag me towards the door.

"This is freaking priceless. Oh, shit, this just made my night," I choked out around my laughs. He'd made out with this girl years ago, but it was only after that we'd doubted whether she was actually a *she* or not. I flicked my eyes over the 'girl' again; I'd forgotten how freakishly tall she was. Obviously, there were a couple of ways we could tell for sure. One way was to check to see if she had an Adam's apple. The trouble was she had one of those fashion scarves wrapped around her neck, so that idea was out of the window. The other way to tell, well, let's just say I didn't like my friend enough to check that way for him. I guess 'she' would always remain a mystery.

Seth frowned and looked at us both like we'd gone crazy. "Where the hell are you two going?"

Ashton gulped, his face pale and nervous. "I think we should go somewhere else; this place looks a little seedy," he replied, shrugging, probably trying for casual but failing miserably.

"Seedy? What the fuck is up with you bitches? Seedy is the best," Seth countered, rolling his eyes. "Nate, come on. First round of shooters are on me," he chirped, rubbing his hands together excitedly and nodding towards the bar. To help my best friend out, I was just about to suggest we go somewhere else, when Seth raised one eyebrow at the girl we were running away from. "Brunette hottie at the bar is mine!" he called, putting one hand in the air to call dibs on her.

My mouth dropped open in shock, and I flicked my eyes to Ashton, seeing he looked just as stunned as I felt. "We are definitely staying,"

Ashton said, nodding excitedly as he slung his arm around my shoulder. I burst out laughing again as Seth straightened his shirt and headed over to make his move.

I was going to die any second. My lungs were going into seizures; I couldn't get enough air. I was laughing so hard I was actually choking on it. Seth, one of my best friends in the world, was throwing up. We were outside the sports bar now; he was throwing up over and over, rubbing his tongue with napkins and shaking his head. Between bouts of vomit, he was mumbling something incoherent about kissing a dude. Mumbling about how, in the bathrooms of the bar, his hand had found something he wasn't expecting when he pushed it up the girl's skirt. It was clear that our suspicions about the girl from Long Beach were correct, and she was, in fact, a *he* instead.

Ashton was off somewhere else, also mumbling incoherently, but no one knew why. Only he and I knew he'd had his own brush with this girl – well, *man*. I would never tell; he'd made me promise seven years ago, and as a loyal best friend, I would take that information to the grave with me. Seth, however, had practically run out of the bathroom, buttoning up his jeans while gagging and running for the door. It was clear what had happened; well, to Ashton and me it was, anyway. This was the best bachelor party I had ever been to, and I would have ammunition over Seth for years to come now.

I bent down and passed him another napkin as he struggled to catch his breath. "Aww, don't worry about it, man. It's happened to the best of us," I teased, winking at him as he shot me a death glare.

"I just felt up a dude!" he whined, closing his eyes and shaking his head.

I laughed some more at that statement and slapped him on the back. "You feel up a dude all the time in the shower, I bet," I joked, nodding down to his crotch. "Really, when you think about it, it's no different." I burst out laughing at his disgruntled expression. Clearly, that hadn't helped in the slightest. "Come on, more alcohol will help," I suggested, motioning with my head for us to go and re-join our group who was standing around chatting in the street, waiting for us.

As we approached, Wayne looked at Seth curiously. "You all right, buddy?" he asked.

Seth nodded uncomfortably, flicking his eyes to me, silently pleading with me not to say anything. I grinned wickedly and threw my arm around his shoulder. "Seth just ate something he shouldn't have," I joked. Seth groaned at the double meaning in my words.

Wayne looked at him and smiled sympathetically. "It was the fish bowl; made me feel sick for a while, too."

I grinned at Seth and nodded in agreement. "Definitely the fish bowl," I teased, winking at him, making him groan and close his eyes.

The next bar was much better. Music played lightly in the background and re-runs of last weekend's football games were playing on the big screen. Unlike the last bar, this one was crammed full of people. Luckily, we managed to get a table at the back, so we'd been sitting around drinking and laughing for the last hour and a half. My dad was swaying on his feet and shouting instead of talking when he got up to purchase the next round of drinks.

I smiled wickedly when I spotted that he'd left his cell phone on the table. This was too good of an opportunity to miss. I laughed as I grabbed mine out of my pocket, quickly opening my music and finding the song I wanted. It was an older song, but it was perfect for this job. I blue-toothed it over to his phone and then set it as his ringtone, turning the volume as loud as it would go. Then I put his phone on the table, pretending nothing had happened just as he came back with a tray full of drinks. He grinned and slid the phone back into his pocket. I waited a little while before calling him.

Kelis' 'Milkshake' started blasting in his pocket. The conversation stopped around us as everyone turned to look at him curiously. I bit my tongue and tried not to laugh as my dad just looked around oblivious, not having a clue it was his cell phone ringing.

"Evan, seriously? 'My milkshake brings all the boys to the yard'?" Ashton choked out, shaking his head. My dad just frowned in response and looked over his shoulder as if searching for where the offending song was coming from.

I choked on my laughter and quickly turned it into a cough as all the boys started verbally abusing him for having that song as his ringtone. My dad shook his head, looking confused as he slid his hand into his pocket, pulling out his ringing phone. His eye flicked to me, an accusing look on his face as he thrust his phone at me. "Change it back, Nate. You know your mother can't stand Kelis," he stated.

I laughed harder as took the phone. "I love how you assume it was me straight away," I said, rolling my eyes jokingly.

"It was either you, Tweedledee, or him, Tweedledum," he replied, nodding at Ashton with a fond smile.

Ashton shot him a mock-offended look. "How come I have to be the dumb one? Your son's the blond!" he protested, laughing as he ruffled my hair.

My dad laughed and ran a hand through his own blond hair. "Don't knock blonds," he scolded, winking at Ashton.

I fiddled with the phone, pretending to change it back, knowing he wouldn't know how to do it himself. My dad was a great guy, but technology wasn't his strong point. I shook my head, frowning, pretending to be confused. "I can't seem to change it," I lied, holding the phone to Ashton. "You ever seen a menu like that? It's not giving me the option to remove the song."

He smiled, catching on immediately as usual. Sometimes we were almost like one person because we always seemed to know what the other was talking about, and most of the time could even finish off each other's sentences. He flicked through the phone, too, before shaking his head. "I can't do it either," he agreed, shrugging.

My dad's eyes widened in horror. My mom seriously hated Kelis; she disliked both her voice and her songs. She would probably smash his phone if it started ringing with that on there. I made a mental note to ring him tomorrow night when they would be asleep. That would be awesome if my mom was woken by that blasting in her ear. Actually, tomorrow was my wedding night; I'd have to have Ashton call my dad for me instead. I was planning on being busy all night long tomorrow consummating my marriage. I sighed happily at the thought; I couldn't freaking wait for the consummating to start.

"Oh, God, you *have* to get it off!" my dad cried, wincing. "If your mother hears that, I won't get any for a month!" he complained.

Ashton and I both groaned at the thought, and I pushed the phone across the table to him again. There was no way I was taking it off there now. Let him go without for a month because parents shouldn't be doing that kind of thing anyway, it was nasty!

"You're a sick, sick man," I scolded, shaking my head and downing my drink as an image of what I had once caught them doing started to flood my brain. I shuddered, and my dad just started to laugh, and laugh and laugh. I made a mental note to make ALL of my friends call him one at a time tomorrow night.

We stayed in the bar for another hour. By then it was half-past eleven, so we decided to head for a club. George was whining and whining that he wanted to dance, so, just to shut him up, we were going to find somewhere to do that. I just thanked my lucky stars that they seemed to know I wouldn't want to go to a strip club tonight. No one had even mentioned it, probably because I'd made it crystal clear to them in the run-up to tonight that the only one I wanted to see shake her little ass was my future hottie wife. No one would match up to her anyway, so why even bother looking?

As we left the bar, for some reason they were all exchanging little smiles and nods. Someone passed one of the duffle bags to George, who snorted a laugh and covered it quickly with a cough. I flicked my eyes to Ashton, wondering what was going on. My best guess would be that I was going to have to wear something even more embarrassing than a Zorro outfit. I was waiting for the pink tutu to come out of the bag and the princess crown or something. Maybe a shirt pinned with condoms? I knew I wouldn't get off with just the Zorro outfit and a vibrator glued to the hand.

My suspicions were confirmed as soon we stepped outside. I was literally grabbed by a bunch of them. I frowned, wondering what on earth was going on, until they shoved me into a dark alley, grinning at me wickedly. George dropped the bag onto the floor, unzipping it deliberately slowly, and rummaged through it teasingly before pulling out a razor and a can of shaving foam.

Instantly I knew what was coming. "Fuck!" I hissed.

I should have expected this. It was my own fault, too – I'd done this exact same thing to Ashton on his bachelor party; I should have guessed he'd want payback.

I backed up and shook my head, holding my hands up innocently. "Guys, guys, can't we talk about this?" My voice came out a little strained as I looked around, mentally assessing my chances of keeping my pubic hair. We were in a dark alley; the walls were brick, no fire escape ladders or doors were coming to my aid. My only chance was to bowl over a couple of my friends and run, screaming, towards the street. I really didn't like my chances of this at all.

Ashton laughed and shook his head. George was swishing the razor around playfully, giggling like a little girl. "There's nothing to talk about. This is happening with or without your consent," Ashton teased, stepping forward.

I groaned and put up as good a fight as I could, but there were six of them, after all. Two of them were sitting on me, and three held my arms and legs as they all pinned me to the cold, hard floor. I could feel the cool night air whipping around my thighs as they yanked my pants and boxers down.

Wow, if people could see this from the outside! I laughed at how this situation could be interpreted and misconstrued if I didn't trust them all with my life. But the thing was, did I trust them with my dick? George was drunk. Extremely drunk. And he was the one wielding the razor. I groaned and shook my head, silently pleading with him not to do it. *Christ, I really am marrying into a crazy family!* This guy was supposed to be responsible, not shaving his future son-in-law's balls. But then again, 'responsible' didn't suit my dad either, considering he was the one sitting on my chest, pinning my left arm to the floor while he started a chant of, "Shave him. Shave him. Shave him."

Bastards.

George was giggling and wiping tears from his eyes as he pulled the cap off the shaving foam. "Hope I don't slip and really cut it off. That would be a shame, wouldn't it?" he teased, laughing harder. "Better keep still there, Nate. I've been drinking, after all; I already can't see straight. This might hurt a little..." he trailed off, and I closed my eyes, shouting for them to get off but laughing hysterically at the same time.

My humiliation lasted for what felt like hours, but in reality was probably only a few minutes. They let me go, and my eyes shot down to my now clean-shaven balls. I had no idea what Rosie was going to say about this – a conversation about drunken grooming wasn't how I envisioned my honeymoon starting.

"You did a good job there, George. Maybe you should change profession and be a manscaper?" I joked, not knowing what else to say.

They all burst out laughing, and Ashton held his hand down to me and pulled me to my feet. He grinned happily, as I pulled up my pants and shook my head at him. "Now, more drinking," he suggested, looking all pleased with himself. "Try not to itch that tomorrow," he stated, nodding down to my crotch, which was already starting to feel uncomfortable.

I groaned. "You're an asshole," I grumbled.

"Just following your lead, bud. You started that shaving tradition four years ago when I got married; I'm just keeping it going," he replied, winking at me as he dumped the bag and shaving things into the nearby dumpster.

They were all teasing the crap out of me as we were walking down the street. Suddenly, my dad stopped walking, causing Wayne to walk into him, both of them stumbling and almost falling to the floor.

"Oh, my God, I need one!" my dad cried, pointing to his left. I followed his eyes and felt my mouth drop open in shock. He was pointing at a tattoo parlour.

"Dad, seriously? No. Come on," I encouraged, rolling my eyes and starting to walk again.

He shook his head fiercely. "I've always wanted one. I'm gonna get it while I'm too wasted to feel it," he chirped. He grabbed George's hand and practically skipped into the door. I burst out laughing and followed him in there. This was going to be classic. My mom hated tattoos; she was seriously going to kill him tomorrow.

While he was in there talking to the guy who was covered in artwork, George was shifting from one foot to the other, looking impatient. When my dad finally stopped talking, George leant in and started speaking to the guy. The tattooist and my dad were laughing; George was nodding in confirmation. I frowned, wondering what was going on. My dad slapped him on the back, and they both disappeared behind the curtain with the guy.

"What's George doing?" I asked, plopping down in one of the plastic chairs, taking the bottle of whiskey they were passing around. I took a swig and passed it on to Brad, wincing as I swallowed the amber burning liquid.

"Maybe he's gonna hold your dad's hand. What's he getting anyway?" Brad asked.

I shrugged. I never knew my dad wanted a tattoo at all; I had no clue what he was going to come out with. "No idea."

It took just under half an hour; obviously, they were fast workers. The curtain pulled back, and both George and my dad limped out, laughing and grinning to themselves. I sighed and raised one eyebrow expectantly. My dad grinned and turned his back on me, pulling down his Iron Man shiny red pants to show me a bandage on his butt cheek. *Oh, God, do I even want to see this? Please, please, do not let my mom blame me for this!* He pulled the bandage down and as soon as I saw the two little words, I burst out laughing.

'Dawn's Bitch'

Yep, my dad had seriously had that tattooed on his ass. He was a dead man walking.

"Show them yours!" my dad enthused, slapping George on the stomach, nodding to us excitedly. *Yours? Oh, crap, he's had one, too?* George grinned and pulled down his purple velvet pimp pants, showing us a bandage on his butt cheek, too. I groaned, fully expecting to see 'Tracy's Bitch' inked there. Instead, when he pulled down the bandage to show us what he'd had done, I literally fell off my chair; I laughed so hard.

My father-in-law had two words inked onto his ass, too. Not the same as my dad's though, like I was expecting. Instead, his were encased in a red circle – a traffic sign, to be exact.

'NO ENTRY'

He'd had a red and white 'no entry' sign tattooed on his ass. Priceless.

Chapter Three

"Gosh, damn, motherfudgeing crapballs on toast!" George shouted.

I laughed and shook my head. He'd been trying to sit down for the last couple of minutes, but every time he got his freshly-tattooed butt cheek to touch the seat of the bus, he screamed like a little girl throwing a tantrum over a new dolly that she wasn't allowed. It was fucking hilarious. My dad was grinning and bearing it, sitting there with a pained expression on his face, trying not to move as the bus bumped down the road. George, on the other hand, was being forcefully pushed into the chair by Brad and Wayne, who obviously thought that his screaming weird expletives in a high-pitched girly voice was the funniest thing they'd heard all year.

"I thought you freaking well said we'd be too drunk to feel it!" George growled at my dad, shaking his head incredulously.

My dad shrugged. "I thought we would be. Don't worry, next bar will sort that right out," he replied, hissing through his teeth as we hit a pothole, making him jump in his seat.

I nudged Ashton. "We so should be videotaping this. Pure awesomeness."

He grinned and nodded, pulling out his cell phone and standing up to record it. Suddenly he gasped and his eyes widened. "STOP THE BUS!" he shouted suddenly, making everyone jump.

I was thrown forward as the driver slammed on the brakes, my shoulder colliding with the seat in front of me. I heard George and my dad cry out in pain as their ass cheeks must have chaffed. The bus screeched to a halt, and everyone turned to look at Ashton, who was currently three rows ahead of where he was standing before the emergency stop.

"Dude, what the hell?" I cried, rubbing my shoulder.

Ashton turned to me and grinned challengingly. "Rematch."

Rematch, what the heck is that about? "Huh?" I mumbled, pushing myself up to standing. There had to be some sort of emergency for him to just

51

shout 'stop' like that. People were driving around us, horns blaring now because we were stopped in the middle of the road. My friends and father-figures were pushing themselves up, glaring at Ashton as they groaned and grumbled under their breath.

"Taylor, are you high?" I asked, shaking my head, still wondering what was going on.

"Rematch," he repeated, raising his hand and tapping the window of the minibus. I followed the direction that he was pointing and frowned as I spotted a mini-golf course on the side of the street. "Re-freaking-match. I'm gonna kick your ass at mini-golf. This is my thing. You guys are going down!" he cried excitedly whilst already stalking off the bus with a confident strut.

I looked at his back to see if he was serious or not. A couple of months ago we'd all gone out for a round of golf. Ashton, being super competitive at all sports – but apparently useless at golf – took the whole thing way too seriously. We'd all teamed up to kick his ass. We'd even paid one of the caddies to move his ball and stuff while he wasn't looking. We'd teased the crap out of him all day about it. I'd heard through the grapevine that he'd been getting lessons since then and was going to request a rematch at some point. I guess he'd decided that hitting a ball into a clown's mouth was a sufficient payback for the weeks we'd called him 'hole in none' after that little incident.

I raised one eyebrow and followed him off the minibus, ignoring people whining behind me that they wanted to drink some more. George was begging for some more alcohol to 'soothe the burn on his delicate little ass'.

When I got to Ashton's side, he was frowning and pulling on the obviously locked metal gates of the mini-golf course. "Looks like you'll always be a loser in that respect," I joked, nudging him with my shoulder.

"Maybe I could make a call and get them to open up for us or something?" he suggested, pulling out his phone and looking around for a number to dial.

"Are you totally serious about this, Taylor? Why don't you just let it go and admit you'll never match up to me in anything that you do?" I teased, smirking at him.

He raised one eyebrow at that. "Batman is superior to Zorro in everything," he answered cockily.

"Except golf and riding horses. Zorro *owns* horse-riding," I joked.

He frowned and kicked the fence in frustration. I sighed and looked up to the top of the ten-foot-high chain link fence. We could easily scale it. Well, most of us could; I wasn't sure about the tattooed versions of Iron Man and Pimp Daddy.

"Loser has to do a forfeit. No backing out, what the winner chooses goes, and it *has* to be done no matter what. Deal?" I offered. There was no way I was losing at any sport, even in the complete darkness and half cut.

"Is there another one near here?" he replied absentmindedly. I shook my head and didn't bother answering as I gripped hold of the cold metal, catching my foot in one of the little diamond shapes and starting to climb it. "Nate, what are you doing? Breaking and entering? I could arrest you for that," Ashton scolded playfully.

I smiled down at him challengingly. "Last to the top has the smaller dick," I called, laughing as he practically jumped on the fence in a bid to get to the top first. *Competitive bastard.*

We were both laughing as we reached the top at the exact same time. Just as he cocked one leg over the fence, I gave him a little shove, making him slip and drop down to the ground on the other side. He landed on his feet with a thump before falling on his ass, laughing and grabbing my ankle, pulling me down, too.

"Guys, seriously, it says there's a guard dog," Seth said, wincing. He hated dogs.

I rolled my eyes, pushing myself up and holding down a hand to help Ashton up to his feet. "Get your ass over here, Seth. All of you. Let's go show this loser not to play golf with the big boys," I ordered, grabbing Ashton into a headlock. We were both laughing quietly as we play-fought and walked towards the start, trying to be quiet on account of us trespassing on private property.

By the time we got to the little storage shed where the equipment was stored, I was convinced this was a bad idea. There was a big padlock on the door; there was obviously an apartment on the grounds where the guy slept above the little store where you paid. I was pretty sure twelve guys breaking and entering and having a drunken game of mini-golf at stupid o'clock at night were going to get caught. But the more drunken part of me really wanted to see Ashton try to win. He would get that serious expression on his face, and I couldn't resist ripping the crap out of him for it.

For some reason, Seth always carried a little Swiss army knife in his pocket, so he was immediately picking the lock of the little store so we could get our clubs and balls. I sighed and closed my eyes as they all gave him a little cheer after a couple of minutes; obviously, he'd managed to get it open.

"Guys, seriously, why don't we just hang a steak from our pants and whistle for the dog to come and get us?" I suggested sarcastically. I laughed quietly when Seth jumped and looked around with wide eyes.

"Will you stop talking about the damn dog?" he hissed, punching me in the arm.

I shook my head at him. "They won't have a dog. Every business in the country has a 'beware, guard dog' sign hanging on their fence. This is a golf course, why would they have a dog?" I mocked, pushing him into the store first. "Oh, my God, Seth, look out!" I joked, looking behind him. Ashton immediately started making a growling sound as Ryan grabbed Seth from behind, making him literally shriek like a little girl.

We all practically fell over laughing before composing ourselves and shushing each other drunkenly. Everyone found a club, and we staggered to the first hole, I waved my hand in a 'go ahead' gesture to Ashton, but he shook his head. "Nope, I'm going last. Age before beauty," he joked, winking at me.

I raised one eyebrow. "Pearls before swine," I replied, smirking at him and stepping up to take my turn. As it turns out, playing mini-golf drunk and in the dark wasn't as easy as we first thought. Luckily, we had a spare bucketful of balls because I had already lost three on my first hole. Ashton was leaning against the wall, smiling cockily at us.

"You had some lessons or something? What's with the grin?" I asked, nodding at his confident pose.

"I might have had someone show me a thing or two," he replied, shrugging.

I narrowed my eyes at that. Ashton was a celebrity in his own right, with a ton of money; I had a pretty good idea he would have had a lot of lessons, not just a couple. "Who?"

He shrugged dismissively and stepped up to take his turn. I watched as he settled himself on the fake grass, positioning his little red ball, holding his club properly and adjusting his feet. He had his concentration face on before he looked up at me and smiled. "Tiger Woods is a pretty good teacher," he stated, just before he pulled back his club above his head, preparing to take a proper swing. My mouth dropped open in shock. Clearly, he'd forgotten we were playing *mini*-golf.

"Ashton, what the-" but I didn't get a chance to finish my sentence because he swung his arm down, whacking the ball so hard it made a resounding crack as the club made contact with it.

Everyone ducked as George cupped his mouth and cried, "Four!"

Time stood still as we watched the ball fly out of sight.

Then all hell broke loose.

Glass smashed. Lights went on in the apartment. People shouted. The boys all burst out laughing. And somewhere nearby, a dog started barking – which of course made Seth scream and run like Jack Sparrow, arms flailing above his head, towards the exit.

"Well, that wasn't meant to happen," Ashton said, standing stock still, staring in disbelief towards the obviously-broken window of the owner's apartment.

"No shit, Sherlock!" I laughed, throwing my club down and running without waiting for him.

I could barely move for laughing. My legs kind of refused to work as I ran for the exit. I was watching Seth as he climbed the chain-link fence in record time. I'd never seen him move so fast. That was a classic fight-or-flight reaction, and he flew pretty damn quickly!

I could hear Ashton laughing behind me; pretty much everyone had already run. I breezed past George and my dad who were half-running, half-limping towards the exit, both of them clutching their asses and laughing painfully.

By the time I made it to the fence and climbed it, the dog was in sight. It was gaining on Brad who was bringing up the rear, complaining he had a stitch as he clutched at his side. The dog was tiny; it had to be some sort of half-breed, rat-type thing. Guard dog it sure wasn't.

I nudged Ashton as he dropped to the floor next to me a couple of seconds before my dad and George hit the ground and took off for the minibus. Half of the people were on the minibus already, which was started and ready to pull away, so we didn't all get arrested.

I cupped my hands around my mouth. "Brad, move your ass, the dog is gaining on you!" I shouted.

Ashton joined in the fun, too. "Christ, Brad, it's huge! Run faster!" he shouted with mock horror.

Brad's eyes widened as he started to turn as if he was going to look over his shoulder at it. "Look where you're going. If you fall, that thing is losing its teeth in your ballsack!" I shouted, laughing at the end as Ashton choked on his laughter.

Brad was almost crying, clutching at his side as he pushed himself on towards us. He jumped the last few feet, scaled the fence like Spider-Man on speed and dropped heavily down to my feet, panting and gasping for breath as he clutched his side in agony. I could barely breathe as he turned his head in the direction of the little brown Chihuahua that was barking its head off and trying to dig its way under the fence so it could lick us to death.

"You assholes! It's not even a fucking dog! Look at that thing; I've seen rats in my apartment bigger than that!" Brad cried, shaking his head in disbelief as he aimed a kick at my shin. I laughed harder and managed to jump back in time so the toe of his boot just breezed past my leg.

"That was awesome. Oh, man, we *so* should have recorded that; we could have put that on YouTube next to the one of George jumping out of that plane!" I choked out, shaking my head at the hilarity of it. This bachelor party was awesome. "You know, they should make a movie out of my bachelor party. The Hangover, part four," I mused, grinning.

Ashton laughed. "Bradley Cooper would play me."

I raised one eyebrow. "You do know he was once voted 'world's sexiest man', right? Therefore, if he's playing anyone, it'll be me," I countered, shoving him playfully.

Ashton rolled his eyes and jumped on my back, almost making my legs buckle with the weight and the drink I'd already consumed. "So that would make me the one who loses his tooth?"

I nodded in response and turned for the bus with him still clinging to my back like a child. "Yep, and Brad gets to be the hairy one," I teased, winking at Brad, who shot me a dirty look.

"You sure you should be getting married tomorrow, Nate? I swear, you two and your bromance thing you have going on, sometimes I wonder, I really do," he stated, looking at Ashton and I suggestively.

I shrugged, making light of it. This wasn't the first time someone suggested Ashton and I should get it on, and I was pretty sure it wouldn't be the last. I was comfortable enough with my sexuality to brush that remark off. "Taylor's not in my league. If I was gonna experiment, it would be with someone worth my attention," I joked, elbowing Ashton in the ribs, making him drop down off my back.

"What? No way. You couldn't do better than me. If we were to get together, then we'd be like the perfect couple," Ashton stated, frowning and looking at me seriously.

I looked him over; even I knew he was a good-looking guy. I guess if I absolutely *had* to bat for the other team then he would probably be my ideal guy. "I guess," I admitted. "We would make one hot couple."

He nodded in agreement before both of us frowned and looked away. "Okay, this conversation has gone far enough. I need a drink," he suggested before throwing his arm around my shoulder and practically dragging me to the minibus.

As we pulled away from the side of the road, I could hear sirens in the distance. Obviously, they'd called the cops thinking they were getting robbed or something. I metaphorically crossed my fingers, praying this night didn't end in a high-speed chase. Rosie would not be pleased if I used my one phone call to call her and tell her to come bail me out of jail the night before our wedding.

Thankfully, we managed to get away before the cops showed up. No one had actually seen us there, or the minibus we were driving in, so I was pretty sure we'd made it. Ashton had already said he was going to anonymously send them some money tomorrow so they could fix their window he'd smashed.

61

As we headed into the latest bar, which we made sure was a long way from the scene of our crime, a pretty blonde waitress sauntered over to our table. I watched as her eyes surveyed the group of twelve rowdy superheroes who sat in her section. I could practically see her unease because she thought we were going to cause trouble.

"Hi there, guys. What can I get for you?" she asked.

Rick was sitting with his back to her, so he hadn't seen her approach. He turned in his seat, and his jaw nearly hit the floor as he leered at her – and not in the discreet way, either. I was actually surprised he wasn't drooling on her shoe. I must admit, she was pretty, but no girl ever compared to my Rosie so I didn't even bother looking, really.

"Holy crap. Wow, you are... wow. I mean, no... it's... I'm... no... but... crap," Rick stuttered before frowning and turning his back on her. She looked a little taken aback as she blushed and looked at the back of his head as he practically squirmed in his chair.

I laughed quietly. Rick was terrible with girls. He wasn't a bad-looking guy, but he just had no confidence at all. "Can we get a round of tequila shots and a beer each, too?" I asked. She nodded politely, shooting the back of Rick's head another glance and sauntering off towards the bar.

"Wow?" Seth teased, nudging Rick, who leant forward and banged his own head against the table a couple of times.

"Why do you guys let me talk to girls? Seriously, I should just never talk to a member of the opposite sex again," he whined. "That was so embarrassing! Can we leave?"

My dad shook his head quickly. "I need to rest my ass a little while."

We all laughed and talk turned to why they had chosen the tattoos in the first place. When my dad started going on about how in love with his sexy wife he was, I tuned out and pretended I was adopted.

When the waitress came over again, Rick looked anywhere but her. He looked beyond awkward. I raised my glass. "To more drinking?" I offered. They all cheered and chinked their glasses against mine in a toast.

"And more dancing," George added as he tapped his glass on mine.

An hour later and my face was starting to get numb. I'd had enough of drinking already. It was after midnight and we'd been drinking for hours. If we kept this up, I was pretty sure that one of us would need our stomach pumped before the sun rose.

"I'm telling you now you can't drown a freaking goldfish! Goldfish can't drown, you idiot!"

Seth cried, shaking his head as he walked back from the bathroom with Rick staggering behind him.

"I did! I put my hand in the tank, stroked its back and it freaking drowned! I'm a fish murderer!" Rick stated, frowning sadly.

Fish murderer? Christ, I need to stop that boy drinking, because he's going to burst into tears and wail about how he hadn't been laid in weeks if he carries on. That was his usual pattern. It started with gibberish and stuff that didn't make sense, moved on to the impossible – hence, drowning a fish – then later came the crying.

"Someone buy him a coffee!" I called at exactly the same time Seth did.

Ashton laughed and shook his head wickedly. "No one's having coffee tonight. I just ordered another round of drinks!" he chirped, picking one up and waving it at Rick, trying to tempt him. Ashton grinned and turned back to me as Rick downed the shot. "I told Anna I'd make him puke tonight," he said.

"That's funny, because she made me promise the same thing about you," I joked.

Half an hour later and we'd had two more drinks. The waitress had just taken our order for another. The whole time she'd been at our table, she kept flicking little glances at Rick but, by the look of him, he hadn't even noticed.

When she walked away to place the order, I nudged him in the ribs. "Dude, what's wrong with you? She's giving you the come on!" I hissed, looking at him like he was stupid.

He frowned. "Who was?" he asked. I rolled my eyes and nodded towards the hot blonde waitress who he'd embarrassed himself in front of earlier. His frown deepened as he shook his head forcefully. "No way, she's like a goddess," he protested.

"Talk to her," I insisted, sitting back in my chair as she sauntered over with a tray full of alcohol. I nodded encouragingly at Rick, kicking his foot under the table, but maybe I'd done it a little too hard because he yelped and jumped in his chair before he composed himself quickly when everyone looked at him.

"I've put these on your tab, okay?" the girl said, smiling a friendly smile.

Ashton told her that was fine, and I motioned with my head for Rick to talk to her again, but he looked like he was struggling to remember how to string together a coherent sentence. I rolled my eyes and turned back to the girl just as she was about to walk off.

"Excuse me. I was just having a little bet with my friends and I wondered if you could help me out with it. I said I'm the hottest guy in the bar tonight, but they don't believe me, so I just wanted to get a girl's opinion. Am I, or am I not, the hottest one from my group of friends?" I asked, raising one eyebrow curiously. I crossed my fingers and hoped this wouldn't backfire and she wouldn't start hitting on me or something.

Her eyes flicked to Rick; a blush rose in her cheeks as she shrugged. "I don't think you are," she answered.

I faked shock. "You're kidding me! So you're more attracted to one of my friends than you are to me?" I asked, shaking my head with mock disbelief.

Again, her eyes flicked to Rick for a split second as she nodded. I kicked him under the table again, and he choked on his drink that he was nursing. He literally spat it everywhere, spraying my dad who was sitting opposite him in the booth. I burst out laughing as he continued to choke. Whiskey even dribbled out of his nose. The waitress gasped and patted his back, looking at him worriedly. Everyone ignored my dad, who jumped up and was practically shrieking like a little girl while rubbing his face with his hands, wiping the drink away.

"Oh, my gosh, are you okay?" the girl gasped, fussing over Rick, wiping his chin with a napkin as he struggled to catch his breath.

He nodded. "Yeah. Don't worry, I do this all the time," he croaked.

"Smooth," I muttered, rolling my eyes.

The girl burst out laughing, and everyone at the table flinched. She must have had the most annoying laugh in the world. It was loud and shrill, like Janice from Friends crossed with a chipmunk wielding a chainsaw.

Rick didn't seem to notice the laugh, though; he just shifted uncomfortably in his seat as she continued to rape our ears with the atrocity that should be recorded and used as a torture device.

"You're funny," she said, smiling at him warmly.

His eyes flicked to me as if he was asking what he should do or say. I nodded encouragingly and willed him to do well. "Yeah, better to play the clown than the... umm... I don't know the rest of that or even where I was going with it," he mumbled, shaking his head and slapping his forehead with his palm.

She let rip another of those atrocious laughs and Seth sucked in a breath through his teeth, shooting me a horrified glance. I just shrugged; Rick hadn't noticed, so that was a good thing.

I tuned out of the conversation, engaging the boys in talk about football so Rick could try his luck without an audience. A couple of times she laughed that god-awful sound, so he was obviously doing well with it.

After ten minutes, he punched me on the arm, grinning like an idiot as he waved a napkin in front of me. "I got her number! Can you believe she's still single? Why on earth would a guy not have snapped her up already?" he asked, shaking his head in disbelief.

Because when she laughs, it sounds like someone is slowly strangling a cat to death? "No idea. Maybe she was waiting to meet her Superman?" I offered, nodding down at his costume. "Anyway, we're about done here, so we're heading to a club so my drunken father-in-law-to-be can bust some moves."

He frowned. "Yeah, maybe. So listen, I can't leave yet, okay? Can we wait like ten minutes or something?" he asked, wincing and looking at me pleadingly.

I raised one eyebrow at that. "Why's that?"

He looked around conspiratorially, obviously checking no one was listening to us, before turning back at me. "My suit is freaking lycra. Not very forgiving in the, er, crotch department, if you know what I mean…" He trailed off, looking uncomfortable as he nodded down to his lap. He moved his arm and I burst out laughing when I saw he had a semi-boner. Looks like the girl had a lot of effect on him in the short time he was talking to her.

"Pervert," I teased, smirking at him.

He shrugged. "She is hot as sin. Can't help my hormones. I haven't been laid in months," he grumbled.

I slapped his shoulder supportively. "Hopefully, that'll change real soon. A lot of girls like playing dress-up," I teased. Now that I'd thought about dress-ups, and I knew we had a few minutes, I decided to sneak off and call my fiancée.

68

"Be right back. I need to drain my lizard," I announced.

I staggered into the bathroom, just needing to hear her voice; I was missing her like crazy. The phone rang a couple of times and then her voicemail kicked in. I sighed as I listened to her message.

"Hey, this is Rosie York, soon-to-be Rosie Peters. Sorry, I can't come to the phone right now, but if you leave a message, I'll call you back as soon as I get done ravaging my soon-to-be husband on our honeymoon." Beep.

I burst out laughing. I closed my eyes and smiled as I spoke to the empty line. "Hey, Stripes. I was just calling to say 'hi' and see if you were okay and still planning on showing up tomorrow. I bet you're giggling too much with your girls to pick up the phone. Tell Anna I'm gonna make Ashton puke and that Rick is well on his way to getting laid by a big-breasted blonde waitress who laughs like a chipmunk that's sucked up a helium balloon, that'll please her." I laughed and shook my head. I could feel the alcohol sloshing around in my system, making me feel a little lightheaded, so I leant against the wall of the stall to steady me.

"So, I'm pretty wasted, I think. Umm... if you're there, then pick up, because I just wanted to tell you that I love you. I'll always love you, Rosie York. Just like in that movie, you know, that crappy one you made me watch the other week... The

Body Guarder or whatever," I mumbled, frowning trying not to think of the horrifying chick flick she'd subjected me to a few weeks back.

"So... you are coming tomorrow, right? Not gonna stand me up, are ya?" I joked, plopping myself down onto the toilet and getting comfortable. "Because I love you, you know that, right?" I mumbled. Then the song hit me, the one from the movie; it suited what I was saying perfectly. "Oh! I got it!" I cried, then immediately burst into song, singing 'I will always love you' – badly – down the phone to her voicemail. I chuckled to myself after a couple of choruses; she was going to tease the crap out of me for that tomorrow! "We should watch that again. Hey, know what they should do? They should make an X-rated version of that movie. Now that would be hot! Ooh, maybe *we* should make the X-rated version. That would be even hotter!" I cried, getting excited, already planning where to get her one of those little metal outfits that Whitney Houston wore on stage. I looked down at my Zorro costume and frowned. "Or maybe you could work Whitney and I could be Zorro? I already have that one," I added, chewing on my lip.

I heard a beep where I had run out of time and I frowned, debating on whether I should just call her back. Maybe she'd even answer this time. I sighed. I guessed I needed to go and see what state my dad and father-in-law were in. I'd probably been in here too long already. Rick must have calmed down by now so we could leave. I stood up and frowned at my costume again. I shook my head at my friend's choice of fun tonight and then proceeded to empty my bladder, swaying on my feet as I laughed at nothing.

As I stepped out of the toilet stall, still pulling the costume back into place, I spotted Ashton, Seth and Wayne sitting on the edge of the sinks. All of them were looking at me and grinning.

Oh, crap, they heard me! How much did they hear?

"Hey, you okay?" I asked, trying to go for casual.

Ashton nodded, fighting a smile. "Yeah. So, you speak to Rosie?" he asked, chewing on his lip as Seth and Wayne giggled like little girls. I nodded, sucking my tongue over my teeth, not wanting to commit to anything. "She get turned on by your terrible singing?" he continued, laughing as Seth elbowed him in the ribs.

I groaned and just decided to go with it. I gripped the side of the cape and whipped it up to cover my face. "If I sing in costume, then hell yeah," I joked, pulling out the fake sword that was strapped to my waist and hitting Ashton on the arm with it.

"Ow! That's not fair, all I have are these stupid freaking bat things!" he whined, pulling out a couple of plastic bats from his utility belt and throwing one at me. It soared over my head and plopped into the toilet bowl. "Whoops, there goes your dad's deposit," he said, laughing wickedly.

I laughed as the boys practically jumped me, forcing me out of the door whilst they sang 'I will always love you' at the top of their voices, making me groan and shake my head as everyone in the bar turned to look at us.

"Time to leave?" I asked, looking at Rick hopefully. He smiled and nodded in agreement.

George jumped up and down on the spot, clapping his hands like a three-year-old girl. "Yay, finally, dancing!" he chirped, wincing as everyone within arm's length of him reached out and slapped the back of his head for embarrassing himself.

Chapter Four

We were play fighting and trying out our newly
learned wrestling moves on each other as we
laughed our way out of the door. Some of the boys
were totally hammered already, stumbling into
things and slurring their words. That was mostly
the ones that didn't come out and drink with us
very much – like Russell, my dad, and of course
George, who I'd found a new found appreciation
for. He was an awesome drunk.

"Guys, what's the time?" I asked. My head
was starting to ache where we'd been drinking for
too long. I either needed to go home and go to
sleep, or drink some more to push past the
headache.

"One in the morning," Ashton chirped, slinging his arm around my shoulder. "And, no, we're not going home yet."

I sighed and nodded. It looked like it was option two we were going for. "Fine. Let's go dance to stop George whining," I suggested, nodding over my shoulder at him.

We headed to a club then. When we were all in and had found a table, we started another drinking competition. This one was word related and quicker than the prank calling we'd done earlier.

"Right then, so I'll start by saying the name of an animal. The next person has to say an animal starting with the last letter of mine. So, for example, I say cat, the next person would have to think of an animal beginning with T. Got it?" I asked, looking at George hopefully.

He nodded, and my dad sat forward in his seat and frowned. "Okay, so you say cat, and I say T?" he asked, looking confused.

Everyone burst out laughing and I shook my head. "Just watch the first few people and you'll pick it up as we go along. All right?" I suggested, winking at him. I turned to Ashton, who was sitting next to me. "Rhino," I started the game.

"Octopus," he replied instantly. We were both pros at all drinking games.

"Siberian Tiger," Brad said proudly.

Russell chewed on his lip for a second before he answered. "Red Panda?"

George winced and looked around for help. "Alligator!" he chirped finally.

Everyone turned to my dad, looking at him expectantly. "T," he said, shrugging and looking seriously confused.

I choked on my laughter and pushed a shot in his direction. "Better luck next time, old timer," I teased.

He frowned. "But you said I had to say T!" he protested, shaking his head fiercely.

Ashton laughed and grabbed his empty bottle of beer. "Let's just spin an empty bottle and do it that way. It's just luck of the draw then," he suggested.

My dad looked at him questionably. "So we've moved onto kissing games now? I like you guys and stuff, but I don't think I'm up for that kind of thing." Everyone burst out laughing at him. If it wasn't for the fact I looked exactly like him, I would be seriously worried that my mom had an affair and I was fathered by someone else.

We played until I started to feel sick. Some of the boys had fanned out and were dancing with a few girls. George, Rick and Russell had been dragged off by a group of girls who thought they were the cutest things ever in their outfits. George was currently laughing and dancing like a wildman as he grinned like a moron. I'd never seen dancing

75

make anyone so happy; maybe he missed his calling in life or something.

I had no idea how long we'd been in the club. I was starting to lose all sense of time completely. There were no windows; for all I knew it could be light outside already. I'd never had so much fun on a boys' night out, ever. I would remember this night forever; I wouldn't class it as my last night of freedom, though, because being married to Rosie was going to be incredible, and it wasn't something I was trapped into. I couldn't wait to marry that hot little brunette. The drink was making me a little sentimental as I gushed to Ashton about Rosie and what an awesome friend he was for marrying Anna, because if he hadn't gotten with her then I might never had met Anna's best friend.

George tore himself away from the group of girls he was dancing with then and staggered over to our table. He smiled lopsidedly at me, and Ashton immediately excused himself to go and dance with Rick and Russell.

George plopped down into the empty seat next to me. "You know that I like you, right?" he slurred, gripping my shoulder and leaning in with a goofy smile plastered on his face.

I nodded in confirmation, trying not to let him push me off my chair while we were sitting there. "I know that, George," I replied.

He smiled and pulled me closer, slinging his arm around my shoulders. "You're a good man,

Nate. I'm glad you want to marry my daughter because she's incredible and needs someone like you to love her and look after her," he cooed. I laughed as he hiccupped in the middle of his sentence. "She's always been my little girl and when I saw her hurt by that asshole whose name will never leave my lips again, I just didn't know what to do. I've never wanted to maim anyone so much in my life. When someone hurts your little girl, it's like they hurt you. You know what I'm saying here?" he asked, looking at me seriously.

I frowned and nodded. "I think you're trying to threaten me in a nice and polite way," I answered.

He burst out laughing and patted my cheek. "I'm not threatening you! I love you! You're like the son I never wanted," he joked, laughing so hard at his own joke that he clutched his side and gasped for breath.

"George, I just can't take you seriously in this pimp outfit," I stated, laughing as his purple hat fell off and rolled towards the dance floor.

He grinned happily and pointed towards the dancing crowd. "I'm dancing again! You coming?" he asked.

I shook my head. "Nah, it just looks like it because of the way I'm sitting," I joked.

He looked at me like I had lost the plot then understanding crossed his face as he burst out laughing, shaking his head. "Looks like... the way

I'm sitting…" he laughed. "You're such a cocky little shit, you really are." He gripped my hand and pulled me to my feet with surprising strength for a man that could barely stand himself. "Don't let your soon-to-be father-in-law make an idiot of himself on his own!" he stated, tugging me towards the dance floor.

I groaned and followed him, dancing and wishing I was back at the table. Especially when he started doing the 'Electric Slide' and the John Travolta pointing thing. When he busted out the running man, I couldn't resist joining in, making him laugh, too, as we started taking it in turns to try and outdo the other. Ashton came over, as I knew he would, throwing down his speciality, which always looked like a cross between the robot and a guy who had just shit his pants. George gave him a 'what the hell' look then flicked his eyes to me, and we both burst out laughing.

"What?" Ashton asked, looking confused as to what we were laughing at. George shook his head, pulling me into a tight hug.

I flinched. *Oh, God, please don't tell me that he gets flirty like his daughter does when he's drunk!* I patted his back awkwardly. He pulled back and cupped my face in his hands. "You are a good, good man. I'm happy to have you in my family. If I have to give my daughter to someone, then I couldn't have picked anyone better than you," he said, his voice breaking through emotion as he put his forehead against mine, sniffing loudly.

I laughed nervously and flicked my eyes to Ashton for help, but he was now standing off to one side trying to teach my dad how to do the 'I've shit myself robot', too. "Thanks, George. I'm happy to be part of the family," I replied, hoping he wasn't going to burst into tears.

He sniffed again and pulled back, his eyes looked slightly unfocused as he smiled at me. He bent forward and kissed my forehead before turning back to my dad and pointing at him. "And, you, Evan Peters! I love you, too! If you hadn't made this guy then I wouldn't be able to call him my son, too," he chirped, grabbing my dad into a hug, slapping his back.

My dad flicked his eyes to me as George clung to him. "What the hell?" he mouthed to me over George's shoulder. I just laughed and shrugged. Rather him than me!

'Moves like Jagger' by Maroon 5 started, and George laughed, pulling back from my dad. "I love this song!" he chirped, putting his hands behind his back and pouting like Mick Jagger as he did some kind of chicken dance. I winced as my dad grinned and started dancing, too. "That's not Mick Jagger!" George cried, shaking his head as Ashton tried to do the leg flick thing. "That's more Michael Jackson; it's like this." He then demonstrated exactly why you shouldn't try to dance like Jagger while wearing tight, purple pimp pants. They ripped at the ass, exposing his red boxers he was wearing underneath. We all burst out laughing, and he just carried on as if he hadn't even noticed.

When it really went wrong for him was when he started the stripping. Stripping was never a good idea in the middle of a packed club, especially while wearing a velvet suit, ripped at the ass, and a chunky gold necklace that said 'Daddy Cool' on it. He gripped his shirt and made a loud growling sound as he ripped it open in an awesome impression of Hulk Hogan. I closed my eyes as he started encouraging my dad to do the same thing.

Oh, God, kill me now! But I couldn't help but laugh at the same time. I was marrying into a seriously crazy family. Suddenly, I heard collective gasps, groans, and gags. "No! That's gross!" Seth cried. I snapped my eyes open to see George leaning over with his hands on his knees. A huge pile of vomit now sat on the middle of the dance floor.

Ashton slapped my shoulder and shook his head. "Your family, you deal with it," he said, turning and walking off quickly. I frowned and wanted to walk away, too, but I guess in situations like this it was now up to me to deal with it. Ashton got off damn lucky with his father-in-law in that respect; I really couldn't imagine President Spencer throwing up on his own shoes...

I patted George's back as he threw up again.
The crowd parted and people stared at us as he
emptied the alcohol out of his stomach. Rosie was
going to seriously kill me if her dad was still sick at
the wedding tomorrow. Damn it, I was in trouble.
But I couldn't help but laugh as I rubbed his back
while he hurled and heaved. No doubt, this looked
awesome to an outsider: a pimp throwing up on the
dance floor with Zorro rubbing his back. *This is the
stuff dreams are made of.*

When he finally seemed to be empty, he
stood up and looked at me apologetically while
rubbing his mouth with the back of his hand. "I got
sick," he groaned.

I laughed harder. "No shit, Sherlock," I
replied, shaking my head at him. "Let's get you
some coffee from the bar," I suggested, wrapping
my arm around his waist.

He smiled at me gratefully. "You're
awesome," he croaked.

I winced from the smell of his breath and
waved my free hand near my face, trying to get rid
of the smell. "Dude, there is nothing awesome
about your breath!" I whined as he carried on
telling me how great I was and how happy he was
that I was marrying his daughter and taking on his
grandson. I pulled a stool up and pushed him down
onto it, waving my hand for the barman to come
over, but he was busy serving down the other end.

I took the opportunity to button up George's shirt for him.

Something patted me on the shoulder. "We need to leave," Ashton hissed in my ear.

I frowned. "I was just gonna get Puking Percy here some coffee," I countered, turning to face him, keeping one hand on George's shoulder to keep him upright.

Ashton shook his head fiercely and nodded over his shoulder. I looked back and what he was motioning at. There were loads of security around, one of them guarding the pile of sick, the others fanning out, obviously looking for the perpetrators. We wouldn't be that hard to find in our choice of attire for tonight!

I nodded in agreement. I didn't want trouble, and it looked like they were going to kick us out anyway. It was always better to walk out on your own two feet than be bustled out by security. I slung my arm around George's waist, pulling his arm around my shoulders as I lifted him to his feet. "Time to go," I muttered.

He frowned. "Are we going to another bar?" he asked, staggering on his feet. Most of the guys had already left and were probably waiting outside for us.

My dad met us at the door, laughing as he looked at George. "You're a lightweight, York!" he chirped, pushing the purple hat back on my father-in-law's head. "Now that your stomach is empty, you can fill it again!" he added, holding out half of a glass of beer to him.

George laughed, and before I could protest, he knocked the drink back in one before holding the glass above his head and shouting, "Booya!"

By the time we got downstairs, the sun was already up. The guys were all joking around in the street, laughing and jumping on each other. Seth was strutting around with a traffic cone on his head singing 'Ding dong, the witch is dead'.

The minibus was still parked where we left it hours before. George literally passed out as soon as we sat him in the seat. My dad plopped next to him and grinned. "I guess we're too old to keep up with you guys," he mumbled. Suddenly he laughed wickedly as he turned back to a passed-out George. "Who's got a pen?"

I groaned and shook my head. "Don't draw anywhere that's going to show up in the wedding photos tomorrow," I protested as Brad started fumbling in the black duffle bags that they'd brought with them. Those things seemed bottomless; they just kept on producing more and more wicked things from there as the night went on. Brad made a triumphant "Ta-da!" as he pulled out a pack of magic markers. My dad grinned and started unbuttoning George's shirt with an excited smile on his face.

I laughed and grabbed the black pen, drawing a very crude drawing of a penis and a face that conveniently had the open mouth where his belly button was. I smiled at it proudly as Ashton giggled and slapped me a high-five.

By the time the boys were done with him, he was more marker pen than skin. I felt sorry for him, but at least there was nothing on his face or neck, so when he was walking Rosie down the aisle tomorrow, no one would know.

My eyes felt heavy from the drink and the lack of sleep. I had no idea what time it was but the sun was up already. I sat forward in my seat and rubbed at my eyes. There was no way I was falling asleep and getting drawn on by these punks!

People were calming down now, settling back into their seats, and it was clear the night was finally over. I breathed a sigh of relief that I had gotten to keep my hair – well, the stuff on my head, anyway. I was also secretly glad it wasn't me who got a 'no entry' tattoo on my ass, because that would have been hard to explain to the little missus on our honeymoon.

"Are we done now?" the driver called over his shoulder. "I was only booked until six o'clock, so am I dropping you guys off at another bar or taking people home now?"

I smiled gratefully that he seemed to have suggested exactly what was on my mind. "Home now, thanks," I called before anyone could suggest one more drink somewhere else. The driver nodded and turned to start dropping people off.

Because we dropped everyone else off first, it took almost forty minutes before we pulled up at Ashton's apartment. My dad, George, me, Ashton and Seth were all sleeping at Ashton's, so we drunkenly staggered up the aisle of the minibus. My dad and Seth both had an arm around George's waist as they headed off the minibus, supporting most of his weight because he was still slightly out of it and was barely able to keep his eyes open. I was about ready to pass out myself.

"Bye, and thanks for driving us. You rock, Mr Driver Man!" I chirped, staggering over to give him a hug, spilling some of my beer down his back.

He frowned and nodded, laughing uncomfortably. "Sure. And good luck with the marriage. I was married once. Didn't work out too well," he replied, shrugging.

"Maybe your wife wasn't as hot as mine is?" I suggested. Then I immediately realised what I'd said. I'd just insulted this guy's ex-wife. *Wow, I need to stop drinking.* I slapped my forehead, which made my ears ring as I shook my head apologetically. "That was wrong. Bad, bad Nate. Sorry. Didn't mean to say that out loud. Not that it probably isn't true because my wife is a hottie, but yeah, I shouldn't have insinuated your ex wasn't attractive," I rambled before slapping my forehead again. *I need to shut the hell up!* I looked over at Ashton pleadingly, hoping he'd punch me just to stop me talking.

85

He smiled and threw his arm around my neck, pulling me towards the door of the bus. "Thanks for driving us around. Excuse my best friend, he gets verbal diarrhoea when he drinks," Ashton stated, laughing wickedly.

I rolled my eyes, and we both crashed into the side of the bus as we tried to climb out together and there wasn't enough room for two to get out of the door. We both snickered, and he shoved me through first, making me stumble and run to catch up with my feet.

I laughed as he practically jumped on my back, his arm way too tight around my neck to be comfortable as he rubbed his hand in my hair, knowing that I hated that. "Can't believe you're getting married tomorrow," he chirped. "Well, actually it's today now!"

I grinned and imagined turning up at the church in a few hours, seeing my little boy walking down the aisle carrying the rings, then seeing the love of my life in what was sure to be a hot wedding dress. *The damn thing had better be hot with the amount we're spending on it!*

I burst into song, singing 'I'm getting married in the morning, ding dong the bells are gonna shine,' at the top of my lungs, which gained us a few weird looks from the few people stupid enough to be out at this time of the morning. Ashton laughed and shook his head, "It's 'ding dong the bells are gonna *chime'*, you dumbass. Not shine!

Why would you be singing about bells shining?" he asked, looking at me like I was stupid.

I frowned. "Really?"

He nodded in confirmation as we both immediately raced for the elevator, practically pushing Seth, my dad and George out of the way as we both jumped in and jabbed the button for his floor at the same time. When the other three went to step in with us, we laughed and pushed them back out, Ashton hitting his fist on the close doors button so they would have to take the stairs.

"No. You assholes. Open the doors! I'm not carrying his heavy ass up thirty-odd flights of stairs!" Seth cried as he practically dropped George and glared at us.

Ashton and I both waved teasingly as the last few inches closed. "Last one to the apartment sucks balls!" I called, winking at Seth jokingly.

Ashton and I both burst out laughing as Seth started banging on the doors to the elevator, dramatically shouting for us to come back. I rubbed my stomach as it growled loudly; I was actually starving hungry now. When was the last time I ate? It had to be lunchtime yesterday. No wonder my vision was swimming.

"You gonna make food?" I asked, looking at him hopefully. At this point, I was past caring that Ashton had to be the worst cook in the world; I would eat anything before my stomach started eating itself.

He nodded and shrugged. "Sure." I followed him down the hallway, both of us knocking on doors as we ran past, knowing that, by the time the occupants got to open it, the other three guys would probably be walking past and would get in trouble. Ashton and I were like little kids when we got together sometimes.

We were both snickering and shushing each other by the time we got to his apartment door. He let us in, and we both headed straight for the kitchen, trying to be quiet because Anna would probably be sleeping. Cameron, their baby, was with their in-laws, though, so at least we wouldn't have to worry about waking him up.

As I rummaged through their freezer, I found chicken nuggets, onion rings, and a couple of frozen microwave meals. I threw them all in the oven and microwaved the meals, standing there with my stomach growling, just waiting to eat already. While I was doing that, Ashton was busy rummaging through his alcohol cupboard, pulling out more bottles and putting them on the side.

"Fish bowl?" he suggested. He grabbed one of Anna's vases from the side, throwing the flowers on the side and tipping the water away. He didn't even bother to wash it properly before he started adding the alcohol, just rinsed it out a couple of times. I winced. There was not a chance I was drinking that.

"Know what we should do? We should get the blender and add some food to it and make Seth drink it as a dare!" I gasped, grinning excitedly.

Ashton looked at me with wide eyes as he nodded, tipping some orange Fanta and Dr Pepper into the vase before adding shot after shot of stuff to it. In their fridge, I found some apple juice, so I tipped that in, too. This one actually looked worse than the one at the bar.

An urgent knocking sounded at the door, so Ashton went to answer it. I laughed as I heard Seth cussing him out, telling him that an old lady had just shouted at him for knocking on her door and waking her up. I grinned and checked the timer on the oven before looking through their kitchen to find the blender. I knew they had one somewhere; we'd had frozen margaritas here before.

Seth trotted into the kitchen, pouring himself a glass from the vase and sipping it before wincing. "This tastes like crap," he groaned.

I nodded. "Know what would make that taste better, buddy?" He looked at me curiously, so I pointed to the oven. "Food." I grinned excitedly. "How about we play dares?" I offered, rubbing my hands together happily.

I really couldn't laugh anymore; my whole stomach hurt. Watching Seth try to drink the concoction we'd made, had almost made me sick, but it was so totally worth it. George couldn't watch it at all; he literally *was* sick. He blamed it on the dare and Seth choking on a lump of unblended chicken nugget, but in reality, he was just expelling more alcohol again. He'd ingested way too much. He was currently dozing on the armchair, clutching a bowl on his lap in case he was sick again. My dad was lying on the floor, trying to fall asleep. Seth was zoned out on his back, whimpering in his sleep and frowning as he mumbled something about not being hungry anymore.

Ashton and I were still sitting on the sofa, laughing about old times. I had my hands behind my head; my feet were resting on their coffee table just because Anna wasn't awake to tell me to move them. Seeing as it was just the two of us left awake, we were playing a game; you had to say the first answer which popped into your head to the other's question.

"Best movie?" Ashton asked.

I thought about it for a split second. "Indiana Jones, Temple of Doom."

"Most fuckable female on the planet?"

"Rosie," I answered without having to think about it.

He laughed and slapped me on the shoulder, looking at me proudly. "That was a great answer. If she was here right now to hear that, then you would be in for a treat, I'd bet," he congratulated, waggling his eyebrows at me. "Best friend?"

"Seth," I joked, wincing as he punched me in the shoulder. "Ow! You little bitch, that hurt," I grumbled rubbing it gently.

Ashton laughed and resumed the game. "Favourite cartoon?"

I frowned. "That's too hard. I'm torn between South Park and SpongeBob," I stated.

He laughed and rolled his eyes at me. "Hottest cartoon character?"

"Ariel the mermaid," I answered immediately, nodding appreciatively.

He frowned and looked at me like I was crazy. "The mermaid? Seriously? Not Jessica Rabbit?"

I shook my head quickly. "No way, I've always had a thing for Ariel. Best Disney movie ever," I assured him.

He laughed and pushed himself up. "Don't let DJ hear you saying that," he countered. I laughed because Ashton was right; my soon-to-be stepson would hate to hear me say that anything was better than Toy Story. Ashton grinned as he walked over towards his wall of movies and pulled out The Little Mermaid, raising one eyebrow.

"Hell yeah, put it on," I agreed eagerly. He grinned and pushed it into the DVD player. As he headed back over to me, he stopped next to Seth and pinched his nose, laughing to himself. After a few seconds, Seth snorted, sucking in a deep breath through his nose and waving his hand in front of his face, still sound asleep.

Ashton plopped down next to me, grinning moronically. The movie started, and we both sat there watching for a little while before my eyes started to get really heavy; I knew I couldn't last much longer. "Thanks for my bachelor party," I said, smiling at him tiredly.

He grinned and threw his arm around my shoulder. "No worries, dude. I'm really proud of you, you know. You've finally grown up and are becoming a man."

I laughed and pushed my empty beer bottle onto the side. "Thanks, Taylor." I pointed at the TV as Ariel was on the full screen. "Tell me that's not hot."

He laughed and nodded in agreement. "Okay, yeah. She's hot, but not as hot as Jessica Rabbit."

"Jessica has bigger tits; that's all it is," I yawned and blinked a couple of times. My vision was getting blurry; I really needed to sleep. "Don't shave my head while I'm sleeping," I mumbled, snuggling down on the sofa to get comfortable.

He laughed. "Wouldn't dream of it," he joked.

I laughed and shook my head. "Ashton, you know I love you, right? In a non-homo way, of course," I mumbled with my eyes closed.

"Yeah, I know you do. Everyone loves me. I'm the best," he replied, yawning.

"No, *I'm* the best," I countered.

"Whatever. Shut up and go to sleep. And, by the way, I love you, too," he stated. I smiled and drifted off to sleep, praying I would wake up with my precious blond hair still attached to my head. The last thing I heard before I fell asleep was George puking into the bowl again – at least, I *hoped* he got it in the bowl.

Printed in Great Britain
by Amazon.co.uk, Ltd.,
Marston Gate.